This Little Tiger book belongs to:

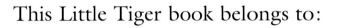

_____

_____

_____

For Annie
~ A.M.

For the Farmhouse Mice
~ T.W.

LITTLE TIGER PRESS
An imprint of Magi Publications
1 The Coda Centre,
189 Munster Road, London SW6 6AW
www.littletigerpress.com

First published in Great Britain 2002
by Little Tiger Press, London.
This edition published 2010

SCAREDY MOUSE

Alan
MACDONALD

★ ★ ★

Tim
WARNES

LITTLE TIGER PRESS

In a small hole behind a closet under the stairs there lived a large family of mice. The youngest was called Squeak. Squeak was a small mouse, a scared mouse, a stay-at-home mouse.

Squeak!

One evening, Squeak was woken up by
his sister, Nibbles.

"Let's go to the kitchen," she said. "I've
just seen something yummy—a chocolate
cake as big as a wheel."

Squeak loved chocolate, but he was very scared.

"What if I get lost?" he worried. "What if we meet the big ginger cat with green eyes?"

"The ginger cat's asleep," said Nibbles. "And I know how to keep you from getting lost."

Nibbles found a big ball of string, and
tied one end around Squeak.

"There," she said. "All you have to
do is to follow the string and you'll find
your way home."

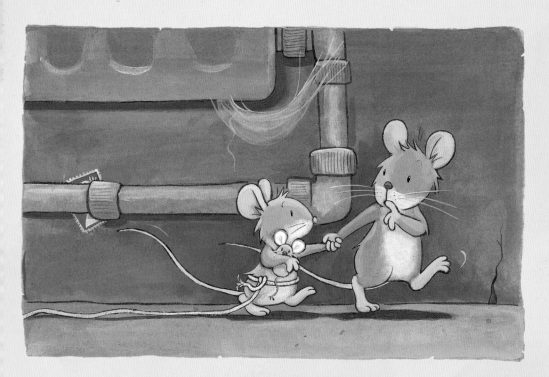

They scurried out of the mouse hole and into the dark, shadowy hall. Squeak kept close to Nibbles, trailing the string behind him. But as they crossed the hall, Squeak saw a long, stripy tail.

"It's the cat! It's the cat!"
he cried. Squeak ran this way and that,
willy-nilly, round and back.
    "Don't be silly," said Nibbles.

Squeak slowly came out of his hiding place.
Nibbles and Squeak scampered through
the dining room, under the table and under
the chairs. But just as Squeak was about to eat
a cookie crumb, he saw two eyes gleaming
in the dark.

"It's the cat! It's the cat!"
he cried. Squeak ran this way and that, willy-nilly, round and back.

"Don't be silly," said Nibbles.

Squeak smiled nervously.

They crept into the den, past the fireplace and past the ticking clock. Suddenly, Squeak froze in his tracks. There, peeping above the edge of the armchair, was a head with two sharp ears.

"*It's the cat! It's the cat!*"
he cried. Squeak ran this way and that, willy-nilly,
round and back.

"Don't be silly," said Nibbles.

"Silly me!" said Squeak.
The two mice tiptoed into the kitchen, across the floorboards and past the cupboard. Squeak peeped inside. He shivered and shook. There, in the shadows, was something furry.

*"It's the cat!
It's the cat!"*
he cried. Squeak ran this
way and that, willy-nilly,
round and back.

"Don't be silly," said
Nibbles.

"Phew!" sighed Squeak.

Just then, Nibbles spotted the chocolate cake on the fridge. It didn't take them long to find their way up to it. Soon their paws and whiskers were sticky with chocolate.

"Yummy," sighed Nibbles. "I could eat all day."

Squeak was a hungry mouse, but also a worried mouse, a scared mouse, a want-to-go-home mouse.

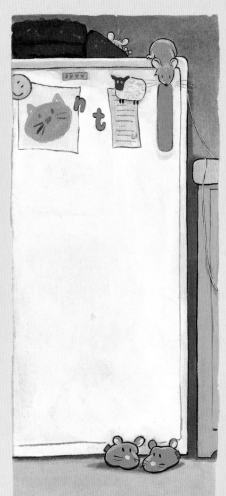

So Nibbles scrambled
down the fridge . . .

and Squeak and the
cake followed.

They heaved the
cake across the
floor, but . . .

just as they reached the door, a shadow fell
across their path.

"*It's the cat! It's the cat!*" cried Squeak.

"Don't be silly," said Nibbles. "It's only . . ."

Squeak ran this way and that,
willy-nilly, round and back.
The big ginger cat narrowed his eyes,
opened his claws and . . .

EEEK!

pounced!

But the cat found himself caught in a web of string. The more he struggled, the more he became tangled . . .

until soon he was tied up
like a fat ginger package.
A mad cat, a sad cat,
a feeling-like-a-fool cat.

Squeak was no longer a small mouse or a
scared mouse. He was a bold-as-a-lion mouse.

And the next time he met the
big ginger cat, he just said . . .